P9-CCW-207

LIVE EACH DAY TO THE DUMBEST

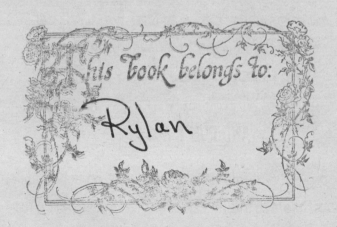

This book belongs to:

Rylan

THINK YOU CAN HANDLE
JAMIE KELLY'S FIRST YEAR OF DIARIES?

AND DON'T MISS . . .

DEAR DUMB DIARY,

YEAR TWO

LIVE EACH DAY TO THE DUMBEST

BY JAMIE KELLY

SCHOLASTIC INC.

If you purchased this book without a cover, you should be aware that
this book is stolen property. It was reported as "unsold and destroyed"
to the publisher, and neither the author nor the publisher has
received any payment for this "stripped book."

Copyright © 2015 by Jim Benton

All rights reserved. Published by Scholastic Inc. *Publishers
since 1920.* SCHOLASTIC and associated logos are trademarks
and/or registered trademarks of Scholastic Inc.
DEAR DUMB DIARY is a registered trademark of Jim Benton.

The publisher does not have any control over and does not assume any
responsibility for author or third-party websites or their content.

No part of this publication may be reproduced, stored in a retrieval system,
or transmitted in any form or by any means, electronic, mechanical,
photocopying, recording, or otherwise, without written permission of the
publisher. For information regarding permission, write to Scholastic Inc.,
Attention: Permissions Department, 557 Broadway, New York, NY 10012.

This book is a work of fiction. Names, characters, places, and incidents are
either the product of the author's imagination or are used fictitiously, and
any resemblance to actual persons, living or dead, business establishments,
events, or locales is entirely coincidental.

ISBN 978-0-545-64258-3

12 11 10 9 8 7 6 5 4 3 2   15 16 17 18 19 20/0

Printed in the U.S.A.   40

First printing 2015

For the Grandmas and Grandpas.

*Special thanks to Kristen LeClerc and the
dumbest team at Scholastic: Shannon
Penney, Yaffa Jaskoll, Emily Cullings, Sarah
Evans, and Abby McAden.*

DO NOT READ
THIS IMPORTANT
HISTORICAL
DOCUMENT

YOU DON'T WANT
YOUR
DESCENDANTS
TO THINK
YOU WERE NOSY,
DO YOU?

KEEP
READING
AND
MAYBE
YOU WON'T
HAVE
ANY

This Diary
Property of

Jamie Kelly

SCHOOL: Mackerel Middle School

GRANDMOTHER: Grandma, also GAMMA for a brief period

GREAT GRANDMOTHER: I don't know

GREAT, GREAT, GREAT, GREAT, GREAT, GREAT, GREAT, GREAT, GREAT, GREAT, GREAT, GREAT GRANDMOTHER:

SOME CAVEMAN LADY I GUESS

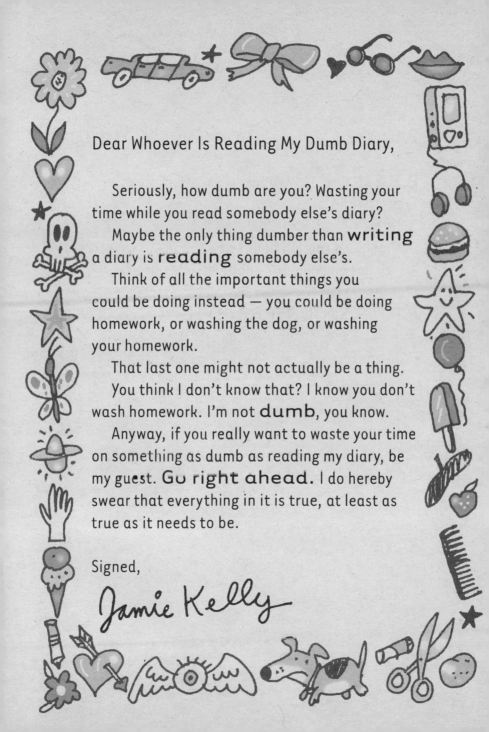

Dear Whoever Is Reading My Dumb Diary,

Seriously, how dumb are you? Wasting your time while you read somebody else's diary?

Maybe the only thing dumber than **writing** a diary is **reading** somebody else's.

Think of all the important things you could be doing instead — you could be doing homework, or washing the dog, or washing your homework.

That last one might not actually be a thing.

You think I don't know that? I know you don't wash homework. I'm not **dumb**, you know.

Anyway, if you really want to waste your time on something as dumb as reading my diary, be my guest. **Go right ahead.** I do hereby swear that everything in it is true, at least as true as it needs to be.

Signed,

Jamie Kelly

P.S. Okay, just kidding. Don't read it.

P.P.S. No, really. I didn't mean it before. **Don't** read it.

P.P.P.S. Is there a limit to how many of these P.S. things you can do? I hope it isn't three.

P.P.P.P.S. DON'T READ IT.

SUNDAY 01

Dear Dumb Diary,

Mom told me to clean the shower today, and I calmly explained that cleaning is what showers already do, so it's **ridiculous** to clean them. "Just go take a shower in it, Mom," I said, adding **"DUH"** because at that moment, it seemed like a good idea.

That moment has since passed, and now she's **also** making me clean my room.

C'MON MOM.

We don't wash the SOAP either.

It washes itself.

You know how when you clean your room you just shove everything into a drawer and push it closed and the room is **magically clean**?

Why don't we design houses so that our entire bedrooms are just huge drawers that we can push closed?

Honestly, when I think of something obvious like this, I wonder if architects are even really **trying** that hard.

It's like my idea for when you're looking in the refrigerator for something to eat and your dad starts yelling for you to not stand there with the door open. If architects were **really** thinking it through, they'd design refrigerators with a back door that dads didn't know about.

SNORT

SNORT

DAD FRUSTRATED
THAT HE HAS
NOTHING TO
YELL ABOUT

SECRET
DOOR

And what about **glitter**? Since we all love glitter so much, why don't we make more glittery food? Who wouldn't like a fantastically glittery sandwich with sparkly ingredients in all sorts of twinkly colors?

Or **fluffy**? Why don't we have more fluffy foods? Fluffy like a kitten. Wouldn't it be great to eat a kitten?

Not like a real kitten but, like, some kind of cake that you could pet and snuggle and kiss and then eat. And it would look like a kitten and maybe meow and chase a laser-pointer dot.

And it would **purr**.

Okay, so purring would make it harder for me to want to eat this cake.

Not **impossible**, but harder.

And what about **clothes**? Everybody knows that there are four main things that are done with clothes:

1. They are loved deeply.
2. They are totally hated right after that.
3. They are thrown on the floor.
4. They are yelled about and washed by Mom.

Don't forget Number 5:
Use old clothes to dress up Beagle

Also don't forget Number 6:
Learn treatment for Dog Bites

But what if we took everything that was so great about my edible kitten technology (and there's **a lot**) and applied it to socks? What if, after you realized that you hated your clothes, you could just **eat** them? Then Mom wouldn't have to yell and you could — I don't know — eat clothes, I guess.

That's not as good as I thought it was now that I see it written out like that.

More genius tomorrow, Dumb Diary!!!!!!!!! Good night.

P.S. How about an exclamation point that means **NINE** exclamation points for those situations where you want to exclaim something at nine times the normal volume but don't have the time to write that many punctuation marks? It looks like this:

Smart, right?

MONDAY 02

TUESDAY 03

WEDNESDAY 04

THURSDAY 05

FRIDAY 06

SATURDAY 07

SUNDAY 08

Dear Dumb Diary,

Grandma died.

That's why I haven't been writing.

It was a week ago. I didn't really know what to write. I think it's the first time I've ever left diary pages **blank**.

When Dad first told me about Grandma, I didn't believe it was true. But then, of course, I realized it's not the sort of thing people joke about:

"Hey, sweetheart, Grandma died. **Just kidding.** Should have seen the look on your face."

Dad was the one to give me the bad news, because Grandma was my mom's mom and she was too broken up to talk about it for a while.

I really didn't know what to tell my mom, which is weird because I've **always** known what to tell people, even when I didn't know and I just made something up. I couldn't even think of a **fake thing** to tell her.

You should have heard me go on and on when my goldfish died. I wonder if people knew I was faking the things I said when my goldfish died.

I tried praying to God about my grandma.

It went something like this: "So, God, I was just wondering if maybe you could **bring Grandma back** and take somebody else in her place, because I'm guessing that you have a certain number of people you need to kill every week or something. I've even made a helpful list here of people that I think might really **enjoy** dying. I can just put it up on the roof, if that would make it easier for you to read from up there. Also, there's a dog on the list, if you would be willing to consider that a fair trade since my grandma was pretty **old**."

Then I suddenly realized how dumb the whole thing was. C'mon, Jamie — the list could get **rained on** up there.

It also occurred to me that maybe it was wrong to ask God to do **exchanges**. Even the mall won't do them without a receipt.

"You know what, God?" I prayed. "Forget it. I'm sure you probably know what you're doing, so I'm just going to, uh, oh hey, I have another call coming in, so I'll have to call you back."

Now, I realize that he might have guessed that I didn't **really** have another call coming in, but I figured he would probably give me a break. I know that **I'd** give me a break, and God has to be way nicer than I am.

Also, if he granted my wish, and Grandma did suddenly walk in the door, it would be hard to not be at least a little **alarmed**.

It could make the funeral super awkward:

"Grandma, it's so nice to have you back, but all of us have to **scream in terror** for, like, an hour now."

Speaking of which, her funeral was last Thursday. There were a lot of people and a lot of flowers.

It kind of made me wonder about the flowers. It's like, "Your loved one died, so we killed these, too."

People told **stories** about her, and shared **memories**, and it was kind of like she was still alive, but not really. It made me think we should share memories of people before they become just memories. My grandma would have liked hearing them.

I also realized that I wasn't really very close to Grandma.

But she was my last one. I'm **fresh out** of grandmas now. No more birthday cards with five-dollar bills in them. No more clothes that don't fit for Christmas. No more conversations about what somebody used to be able to get for a quarter.

25¢

Hey, Grandma, if everybody was so happy getting things for a quarter, why did you all change it?

At the funeral, Dad said that, as time goes on, Mom will be able to pull herself together better, but way deep down inside, a part of her will probably always feel like a **little girl** that lost her mom forever.

Lost. Her. Mom. Forever.

That's when I lost it. I mean, REALLY lost it. You hear people use the phrase KOO-KOO-BANANAS all the time, but I was really crying like koo-koo-bananas.

I don't remember the last time I **cried** like that. I was crying for Mom the most, but also for myself. I cried for Mom's sister, Aunt Carol, who had lost her mom, too.

Then I cried for Dad, because I knew how bad he felt for my mom, and how bad he felt for me because I was crying. And I cried for Grandma, because if she knew she was making us all cry this way, she would have felt **really, really** terrible about it.

I went to the ladies' room and even cried a little for my reflection in the bathroom because I looked so **sad**, but I also couldn't help noticing how **adorable** I looked when I cried. Then I cried for noticing my adorability when I was supposed to be funeral-crying.

Sometimes I am just inappropriately lovely

DAINTY DABS

I cried a little for my beagles, Stinker and Stinkette, because I knew that if they did something like **poop on the carpet** while we were at the funeral, I would have to spank them until I needed to pack my hand in ice.

Spoiler alert: They didn't do it, but I still cried. **I pre-cried.**

But here's the weird thing about crying: Eventually, you just run out of tears.

It's like peeing.

BLIP o BLORP

The next day, I guess it must have been Friday, I didn't cry **at all**. And I didn't see Mom cry, either.

I think we all wanted a day when we didn't talk about it. I thought about talking about it, but Mom was still not herself, so I thought it was better not to say anything to her about anything.

So even though Mom is the one I'd normally go to with beauty questions, I asked Dad if I could get my lip and nose and eyebrow pierced. Then I got a solid **ten-minute lecture** about what should and should not be pierced.

There's a pretty long list of things Dad says I can't get pierced, by the way, including a few that I wouldn't have even thought of. His main point was that there's a lot of beautiful jewelry you can wear that nobody has to **stab** you with.

Glad I asked him before I got it done. Now I know **not** to ask Mom before I get it done.

What my Dad thinks jewelry is

Aunt Carol and Uncle Dan took on the responsibility of going through my grandma's old stuff and packing it up in boxes. Aunt Carol even brought over a box of Grandma's things she thought I might like. I haven't opened it yet, because it just feels **weird** to go through somebody's belongings that way.

I thought about how, one day, Angeline might go through my old stuff and try it on and probably even use my toothbrush and get her **delicate cooties** all over everything. I'm telling you right now, Angeline, if you're reading this, I'm letting the dogs lick my toothbrush THIS VERY MINUTE. Don't feel so smart now, do you?

P.S. I really and truly am doing that.

Also I used my dental floss between Stinker's nasty toes and put it BACK IN THE CONTAINER

SQUEAK SQUEAK SQUEAK

FLOSS

TUESDAY 10

Dear Dumb Diary,

Isabella was **super gentle and kind** to me today about my grandma dying.

(After I convinced her that there was nothing **contagious** to worry about.)

She also said I could probably get out of some homework, since the teachers always go easy on kids for a while if they know that something like this is going on in their lives.

Isabella once used a **stubbed toe** to delay a book report for two weeks, until she could no longer convince the teacher that she needed a healthy toe to read.

Both hands needed to take careful notes...

so healthy toes are required to turn pages

makes sense to me

Isabella also thought that if Grandma hadn't shared a last wish, maybe we could just **assume** it had something to do with Isabella not having to do homework, either. She thought I might like to tell the teachers that.

I told her that there was **no way** the teachers would even know about my grandma. She was sure they would because sometimes parents call and let the school know about things like this, and also, since my aunt works at the school and is married to the assistant principal, the word was probably out.

Sorry, Mom, but Jamie's Grandma said that she didn't want me to eat broccoli again.

My social studies teacher, Mr. Smith — you remember, Dumb Diary, he's the one who wears **fake hair** in order to look like a younger man with a full head of fake hair — actually gave me a sad little greeting card in class today.

"I'm sorry for your loss, Jamie," he said, and he seemed genuinely **sad**.

"What do you mean?" I said.

"Your grandma. I'm sorry you lost her."

A few other people have said the exact same thing to me, but it makes no sense when you think about it. When somebody dies, you don't **lose** them. You know right where you put them, and you know that they're going to stay there. They're not just going to wander off. When somebody dies, it's like the only time you **can't** lose them.

NOW DON'T MOVE

Angeline called it **"passing away,"** as in, "Sorry your grandma passed away."

But that sounds a little strange to me, too. It sounds like "faded away," and if anything, my grandma did anything **but** fade as she got older. If you asked Grandma to wear something nice, you needed sunscreen to protect yourself from the brightness. I've studied the old-timey photos, and my theory is that old people dress in colorful outfits to compensate for all the time they spent in black and white as children.

EARRINGS VISIBLE FROM AIRCRAFT

GOLF BALL-SIZED BEADS

PURSE OR PONY CARRIER?

PATTERN CAPABLE OF CAUSING MILD INSANITY IN MAMMALS

Gray

Gray

Gray

Dark Gray

gray

GRANDMA

GRANDMA AS A CHILD

Anyway, I've been using the word **"died,"** because that's what she did. All the other ways make it seem like I'm trying to make it sound not so bad.

But it **is** bad. I know that, even if some people try to act like it isn't.

I'm not stupid: If dying isn't bad, why are ambulances in such a **hurry** all the time?

And Ambulance Drivers...

WOO WOO WOO

you keep going as fast as you have to

especially If I'm the one that called you

Hudson said something about my grandma, too.

I don't know if I've ever mentioned Hudson Rivers to you before, Dumb Diary. He's the eighth cutest boy in my school. Maybe even **seventh** now, as boy number four went on vacation and made some **questionable** decisions about getting cornrows put in his hair. This, I think we can all agree, has affected his rating. As a rule of thumb, cornrows only work reliably on:

    A. Corn.

    B. People who look good with cornrows.

    C. And that's it.

The rest of you, no. **Just. Don't.**

Dicky Flartsnutt demonstrates an example of who should not get cornrows.

Also his body spray is seriously not working here

Anyway. Hudson said something. It was probably **nice**. I don't remember. I'm not concentrating very well these days. Sometimes I feel like the entire world is like one of those lessons about an early explorer who discovered something like one of the larger hills in Ohio. You know it will probably be on the test, but you just **can't** make yourself care.

Hey, Education. It's hard to care about these things....

GUYS WHO INVENTED THINGS

PIRATE HOOK SHARPENER

NOBODY USES ANYMORE

PEOPLE WHO BELIEVED THINGS

WE NOW KNOW ARE WRONG

THE DATES OF EVENTS

WE WON'T BE ATTENDING

WEDNESDAY 11

Dear Dumb Diary,

I opened the box of Grandma's things today. There were some old photos of her and my grandpa together, and some photos of her when she was about my age.

People used to dress nicer back then. Honestly, if we don't have to dress up for something, my family usually looks like a group of **scarecrows** that doesn't get invited to the places the nicer scarecrows go.

I wanted to ask her, "Why did you all used to dress so nice, Grandma?"

But then I thought, *Oh. Right. You can't give me answers anymore.*

Grandpa going out to mow the lawn

Dad going out to eat

There were some pictures of my grandpa, too — some from when he was a boy about my age, and some from when he was the same age as my dad.

He looked really **tough**, maybe even a little **scary**.

Back then, men like Grandpa would just go out back and kick a few dozen trees out of the ground and build a house from them using only their fists and a rusty saw with one tooth in it.

My dad, on the other hand, sometimes can't open a folding chair without **pinching** a finger off.

I wanted to ask him, "What made you so different, Grandpa? Why were you guys all so tough all the time?"

And then I thought, *Oh. Right. You can't give me answers anymore, either.*

When people die, it's like they set the phone down while you're talking to them, and they never pick it up again.

There was a necklace in the box that I've decided to wear for a while. It's pretty **ugly**, but I believe people really used to like ugly things. I don't think they had as much makeup back then, and the idea was probably that if you wore an ugly necklace, your face would look **prettier** in comparison.

It makes me think that if I wore Stinker around my neck, I could be **on the cover of a magazine**.

It's an interesting strategy, but I think I'll wear the necklace under my shirt. If Mom sees it, it might make her cry, and not just because of its ugliness.

Oh.
One other little thing.
I found my grandma's diary in with her stuff.
I'm thinking about reading it.

Dear Dumb Diary,

Okay. I know that I might sometimes give the impression that I don't want anybody to read **my** diary, although it probably would be okay with me. I don't know. I haven't given it much thought.

But don't you think that my grandma would want me to read **her** diary? Look, here's what it said on the first page:

"To whomever is reading my diary without my permission: DO NOT CONTINUE READING. I wish upon you a thousand curses and a thousand more. Stop now, before you violate my privacy any further."

See what I mean? **It's not exactly clear.** You could take that a lot of ways. I think what she's saying is that I can read it only if I have permission.

And if I didn't have permission, wouldn't she have burned it long ago? That's really the only way somebody can totally deny you permission.

when people feel strongly about something

they should throw it into a volcano

She could have always thrown it into a volcano. I get the impression that there were a lot of volcanoes in those olden times, although I might be thinking all the way back to **cavemanny times**.

The fact that I have the diary in my possession **AT ALL** is obviously permission to read it in exactly the same way that I **CAN'T** read things I **don't** have.

Case closed.

Prettiest. Lawyer. Ever.

They let me use real doves in the courtroom

I HAVE PROBABLY INVENTED THE PROFESSION OF **LAWYERINA**

FRIDAY 13

Dear Dumb Diary,

　　Isabella was **upset** at school today. She admitted that she's been thinking about my grandma a lot.

　　See, some people think Isabella is unkind because of how she used to scare little kids out of their Halloween candy, but they don't stop to consider the **good** Isabella did for the families of the psychiatrists who will treat those kids all the way into adulthood.

　　And they think she was mean for throwing apples at that crabby old retired guy who always yelled at us for walking on his lawn, but they don't ever say anything about how that lucky old guy got a **TON** of free apples. And also four free eggs.

　　And they think it was wrong of her to make up a story about her mean older brothers and tell the police that they —

　　Okay, well, she did give that guy **free apples**.

Anyway, I know Isabella and I know that Isabella **is** kind. This was made even clearer to me when I saw how sensitive she was about my grandma.

Isabella said she has started to worry that, one day, she might be too old to do certain things. She was afraid that she could die and leave behind a lot of people without telling them how **lame** they were.

Isabella said quietly, perhaps even holding back tears, "I don't want anybody left **unpunched**."

ALL PEOPLE HAVE THE RIGHT TO BE SLAPPED AROUND BY ME

I THINK I JUST DESIGNED HER CREST

She asked if I knew anybody that my grandma might have meant to abuse or scratch or something, but never got around to it.

"Or maybe there was a bed of flowers she wanted trampled, or somebody's lawn wrecked? Maybe some hair that should have been pulled?"

See? Isabella's **TOTALLY** kind.

I told her that I had no way of knowing.

Unless.

Unless we looked in my grandma's diary.

If you ever find yourself facedown, staring at the floor of the school hallway, it could be because you also gave Isabella a reason to suspect there was something in your backpack that she wanted AND you had neglected to take the essential step of removing your backpack before you made her suspect that. Rookie mistake.

After some rummaging around, she was **finally** convinced that the diary wasn't in there. I explained that I had it at home, but I hadn't read past the first page because it said that nobody should read any further.

By **"explained,"** I mean **"grunted."** She was still sitting on my back.

That's when I learned that I was inviting Isabella over for dinner.

And into my room.

And into my grandma's diary.

I told you that people used to dress differently than we do now. But I may not have mentioned that they used to **write** differently, too.

First off, they wrote more in cursive, because supposedly it's a faster way to write, even though every single other thing in their whole entire world was slower. Hey, old-timey writers, what was the **big rush**?

"I have to hurry up and finish writing this so I can go sit on the front porch and churn butter without an Internet and watch old-fashioned people walk slowly past in their absurdly clunky shoes."

But let me get back to the cursive writing thing. Have a look at this sentence here:

Quick, let's buy some zebras.

It says, "Quick, let's buy some zebras." That thing that looks like a **2** at the beginning is actually the letter *Q*.

Hey, **old-timey Letter Inventors**, why did you write it that way? Hadn't any other shapes been invented yet?

I'm sure they must have sat around saying, "What should the letter *Q* look like? How about if we just use the number 2? Hardly anybody ever uses a 2 anyhow."

The only reason I can read cursive is that my grandma used to send me long letters and Mom made me read them. Isabella never learned cursive, so she can only read some of the words, which **frustrates** her and is one of the reasons she says she now hates everybody from history. (Also, she hates them because they want to be studied by us.)

"And if those old documents were so important, they would have **typed** them," she says.

But I'll give you a break, Dumb Diary, and I'll write my grandma's diary entries out in a way you can understand.

More reasons Isabella hates Everybody from History

Eyewear designed to improve your vision only somewhat.

They made hats TRIANGLE-SHAPED instead of in HAT SHAPES.

Dressed like they were just DARING you to beat them up.

They could have done less important things, so we didn't have to learn about them.

Here's something else that was different. Grandma didn't **name** people in her diary — she used their initials. I've seen this in other old-timey writings, too.

She wrote that she had a crush on somebody that she called M.B. She didn't even put his name — she just used his initials. She must have been worried about some nosy person getting in her diary and reading it. How **paranoid** can you get, Grandma? **OMG**, nobody is going to read your precious diary. **Relax.**

I wish I had thought of that.

Here's the first entry:

I saw **M.B.** at school today, looking as wonderful as ever. I was prepared to start up a conversation, but just as I approached, **A.S.** slid in and the two of them began laughing and talking. I felt as though I had just faded away.

If I used intitials, I'll bet nobody would know who I was talking about.

Isabella and I agreed that it's **exactly** like something we would write, except that Isabella would have probably pushed A.S. down and I might have slid a piece of salami through one of her locker vents just before a long weekend.

I wanted to yell at her diary, **"C'mon, Granny, stick up for yourself!"**

Here's what another one of the entries said:

Big dance coming up soon. I sure hope I get to dance with M.B. Nothing in my life is more important to me. Hope A.S. isn't there.

If you don't have salami, there are other things you can use...

...or do a super-fun combo!

GARLIC BOLOGNA

DIRTY SOCK

STINKY CHEESE

And then it hit me. It sounded **EXACTLY** like something I would write. And it made me feel a little sick that Grandma was back there, in the past, wasting the time that I know she doesn't have an infinite amount of, since I'm here in her future and I know — well, I know that she doesn't have any time left **at all** now.

I closed the diary and wouldn't let Isabella read any more.

We need a way to call people in the past

and tell them what we think

LAME

Instead, we talked for a while in the dark about the things all girls talk about — music, and boys, and how Angeline will be ugly when she grows up, but I couldn't stop thinking about that entry in Grandma's diary.

It was **so** dumb. All she was thinking about was some dumb dance.

Like the ones I dumbly think about.

Like the one that's dumbly coming up.

Am I dumb, too? Am I back here **right now**, in my own past, being dumb? And are you reading this right now, granddaughter of mine, thinking I'm dumb?

Well, stop it. It's disrespectful of your old Granny. Go spank yourself.

Unless they have robots for that now. Go tell your Spankbot to spank you.

or if you have a TIMEOUTBOT that would be OK I guess

But spanking would be better

SATURDAY 14

Dear Dumb Diary,

Isabella demanded to read one more of Grandma's diary entries before she went home this morning. It's hard to resist when she gives you her **puppy-dog-eye** thing.

Her **puppy-dog-eye** thing goes like this:

"Do what I say or I'll poke your puppy dog in the eye," she says.

So I read her the next entry:

How do I stand a chance against that beautiful hair and those big brown eyes? Sometimes I imagine that a circus elephant would just sit on A.S., and it makes me feel a little bit ashamed of myself, and a bit angry with myself, and a bit fond of elephants, and a bit interested in knowing when the circus is next coming to town.

oh
she'll
do
it

"Where did your grandma go to school?" Isabella asked.

I told her that I had **no idea**. She wanted to ask my mom, but I pointed out that if we did, my mom would probably take the diary away from me, since I'm sure she wouldn't want us to read it.

"**Remember?** That's what happened when you asked her if she knew how to get hair spray off a beagle," I reminded her.

Then I remembered that there was more stuff in the box that Aunt Carol brought over, so we dug through it until we found some of Grandma's old report cards. **All A's in art.** Guess it runs in the family.

Isabella squinted at the fine print.

"Got it. Walker Middle School," she said. "It says it's in Hazel Heights. I wonder if it's still there."

I asked Isabella why she wanted to know, and she told me to mind my own business. I pointed out that business-minding was exactly the **opposite** of what we were doing, and she agreed that I made a good point and rubbed Stinker's chew toy in my face and left.

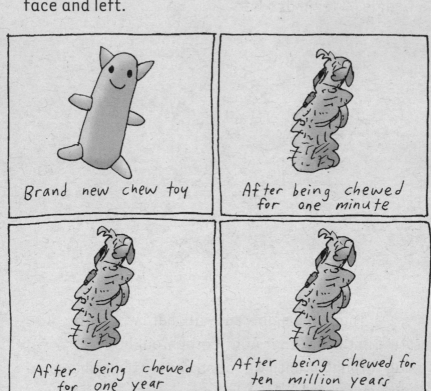

Brand new chew toy

After being chewed for one minute

After being chewed for one year

After being chewed for ten million years

CHEW TOYS ACHIEVE MAXIMUM DISGUSTINGNESS IN ONE MINUTE

SUNDAY 15

Dear Dumb Diary,

    Aunt Carol and Uncle Dan came over this morning and **hugged** me a little longer than usual. I guess people hug when they're sad. But they also do it when they're happy.

    Hugs are actually a pretty unreliable way to know how people are feeling, especially Isabella. She also does it when she's angry and hungry. (Although these do tend to be **throatish hugs**.)

can't we accept that everyone HUGS a little bit different?

Aunt Carol is married to our assistant principal (my Uncle Dan), plus she works at my school, so she knows all the things that are going on at school that the kids permit her to know.

"Are you going to that dance?" she asked.

"I don't know," I said.

"You know who you should go with?" she said.

"Who?"

"Your butt."

This is the type of thing my Aunt Carol says when she wants my mom to throw something at her.

"Carol! Don't say 'butt' to her," my mom said.

"*But* why?" Aunt Carol said in such a way that you could actually hear her using italics on the word **"*but.*"**

Oh, Aunt Carol

My mom said she knew exactly what Aunt Carol wanted that particular "*but*" to sound like, and Aunt Carol said that was because my mom is an **expert** on how butts sound.

As the two of them laughed, I thought about Grandma for a second, and I wasn't sure if it was right for them to have this dumb conversation, considering that their mom was . . . **you know**.

And I think that must have occurred to them, too, because they stopped laughing before they got to the honking-cackling-snorting phase.

I'll know that Mom is officially herself again when her laugh starts sounding like something going **very wrong in a petting zoo**.

MOM LAUGHING

GOAT WITH BRONCHITIS THAT ACCIDENTALLY ATE A CROW

SAME SOUND

Dear Dumb Diary,

Today Mr. Smith probably taught us some things about stuff. I don't really know. Maybe it was one of those lessons I'll need **later in life**. They've been telling me I'd need these school things **later in life** since kindergarten. I'm really looking forward to seeing how the macaroni art comes in handy.

Foolish pretty human! Nothing can stop our ALIEN DEATH RAY!

EXCEPT kindergarten ART PROJECTS!

BRZAAAP —

DO YOU REALLY THINK I'M PRETTY?

... And for her HEROIC bravery, EARTH let her choose her husband and send one enemy to prison.

I was **trying** to concentrate on what Mr. Smith was saying, but he was doing that thing that teachers do sometimes when it's obvious that they don't want you to learn what they're teaching.

They pick something that doesn't matter to anybody and talk about it in this way that makes you think about **anything else in the world**.

You know why they do this? Think about it: It's because if you managed to learn everything they had to teach, you could just steal their job the following year. They really **NEED** you to miss some things.

And so I thought about other things.

I kept thinking about how things were so **different** in the olden times when my grandma went to school. The Internet hadn't been invented yet, and there were maybe three television channels, and I seriously doubt that there were any of the high-quality chewing gums that modern humans require.

The only thing you had to distract you from reading your schoolbooks was reading your not-schoolbooks.

Try to imagine this.

You know how you get impatient waiting ten seconds for your computer to start? My grandma had to wait **fifty years** for hers to start.

Maybe that's why she seemed a little **dumb** to me.

Angeline stopped me in the hall today and asked how I was doing. I appreciated her concern, but I also **resented** it. It made me feel like she thought I was weak, and in the wild, that would mean that she was planning to take over my banana tree or something.

    "You can't have my bananas," I said, immediately realizing that she might not be bright enough to understand what I meant by that.

    It must be hard being so dim-witted.

What makes you think this dumb dirty ape is Angeline?

I never said that this is a drawing of Angeline

"There's another dance coming up," she went on, seemingly deaf to my banana warning.

I wondered just how much dancing the school thought we needed to do. Honestly, you probably only **medically** need to dance for a few minutes a day, so they don't really need to organize a special event for it. I mean, you're supposed to get a lot of vitamin C, too, but we don't have a big orange-juice-drinking party every week.

This was the point when I realized that I wasn't just wondering this stuff. I was saying it. **Out loud.** Maybe even shouting it. Perhaps **damply.**

I shouldn't get mad at Angeline. I know she means well, but for some reason, I always get mad at **well-meaners.** Plus, I know that she is attractive on purpose, and I feel that this is a hurtful action on her part, maybe even a form of nonaggressive and deeply pleasant bullying.

Angeline is INTENTIONALLY wonderful. If she REALLY cared, she'd tone it down.

CLEAN, COMBED HAIR? C'MON

SHE COULD HAVE A CAT GNAW SOME HAIR OFF.

BABY BLUE EYES? AND **TWO** of them? NOT NECESSARY.

HOW ABOUT A NASTY EXPRESSION SOMETIMES? AND CUT OFF THE LASHES.

UNCHEWED NAILS? TAKE A BITE, ANG.

HONESTY **CAN** BE CURED. SNATCH A PURSE OR TWO.

LOOK, WE COULD ALL LOOK GREAT IN OUR CLOTHES. BUT MUST YOU? IT SEEMS MEAN TO US.

GROWING IMMENSE HAIRY FEET WOULD BE A SWEET GESTURE.

"Don't go to the dance if you don't want to," Angeline said, "but we need posters. And you're the best postermaker in school."

She was right. School posters can be disastrously amateurish.

FOOD DRIVE

BRING CANS of FOOD for the HUNGRY

CREAM OF GARBAGE SOUP

your Mom probably has some JUNK you'll NEVER EAT

MOLLUSK EYEBALLS

NAME CALLERS ARE JERKS

WE CAN BEAT BULLYING

PUNCH!

BULLY →

OW

TUESDAY 17

Dear Dumb Diary,

Isabella was in the library on a computer every free minute she had today. I figured she was doing homework, or trying to crash the Internet, or bidding on a boa constrictor.

"They're just like kittens," she always says. "Legless kittens that choke people sometimes. You wouldn't hold it against a kitten, would you, if it had to choke somebody?"

She also thinks spiders are just eight-eyed kittens that can shoot yarn out their Butts

I wish I could forget I drew this

I kept trying to sneak a look at what she was doing on the computer, but the librarians always crowd around her when she's online to make sure laws aren't being broken, so I couldn't see anything.

They actually bring in extra LIBRARIANS from Other schools

I asked her about it later and she just scowled and said, **"Mind your own fat hairy business, nosy,"** which is Isabella's way of smiling and winking and saying, **"It's a secret."**

Isabella considerately reminds us to keep our noses out of her Business please

Because this is the main way noses can accidentally get Bitten

When I got home this afternoon, I read another entry from Grandma's diary:

My best friend, R., says that even though M.B. seems to be attracted to A.S., I shouldn't give up — even if that means giving A.S. a punch in the nose right in front of the entire school. R. says the worst that could happen is that my parents will double my chores and maybe the principal will give me a paddling.

A **PADDLING**? They paddled kids at school? Isabella is probably pretty glad they don't do that at our school.

SPANK

They would play this game with Isabella every single day

I wish there was some way I could send a note back in time and tell my grandma not to be so dumb. Don't you know that you're going to grow up and be a grandma? Stop acting like a **dumb kid**. Stop acting like **me**.

I just don't like the idea of Adults as DUMB LITTLE KIDS

my math teacher

2+2=CAT

my Doctor

my Mom

WEDNESDAY 18

Dear Dumb Diary,

Angeline used her face to bother me today by making sounds come out of it prettily.

"We need those posters for the dance, Jamie. You said that you'd take care of it. If you won't do it, then I'm going to have to find **somebody else.**"

She shook Dicky Flartsnutt at me to make her point.

"Point taken," I said, wondering how Dicky felt about being used as a point.

He just grinned. Nobody wants to be a point, but Dicky seems to enjoy any form of human contact.

And not many of the boys would object to Angeline using them as a visual aid.

It's pretty rude to wag a nerd at somebody

I don't think shaking Dicky Flartsnutt is a good idea. I often get the impression he's already a little **shaken**.

One time he asked me, "Jamie, when I lick my own palm, it doesn't make me scream. But when I do it to a stranger's palm, they always scream. Do you think there's something **wrong** with those people?"

When I got home, I started working on the posters. I've learned that my grandma spent too much time on dumbness like this dance, and I don't think we should dumbly encourage kids to be dumb.

I think **MY** future granddaughter would approve of my reasonable and intelligent posters.

Low Sparkle Glitter

Medium-size poster boards in WHITE ONLY.

Not my Brightest Colors

SONGS I _DON'T LIKE_ that much playing while I work

TAN
BEIGE
LIGHT TAN
GRAY

ONLY PARTIAL TALENT USED

THURSDAY 19

Dear Dumb Diary,

Angeline used a **bad word**. About my posters. Okay, so she didn't think my posters were right for the dance and said that she had imagined that they would be — in her words — "good."

She also said that the idea was for people to **want** to come to the dance, and that my posters looked more like something advertising a *funeral*.

That's right. She said FUNERAL. And then she clamped her hand over her mouth.

I don't know how long after somebody has to go to a real funeral that it becomes okay for you to use the word "funeral" around them, but I'm pretty sure it's **never ever ever ever** again.

Of course, Isabella was **right there** to support me and my posters, which she did by shrugging and wandering away. She probably meant to say, "Angeline, you horrible smear of insensitivity, stop being cruel and blond."

I told Angeline that she gave **me** the responsibility for the posters, and I'm not going to change them.

She nodded and backed down, although I know it's only because my grandma died and she felt awful for accidentally using a bad word on me.

Maybe we need better words for funerals.

"Grandma is celebrating her FIRST UNBIRTHDAY PARTY."

G-MA

"Grandma is winning the breath-holding contest!"

"Grandma had to catch a flight."

FRIDAY 20

Dear Dumb Diary,

Another entry in Grandma's diary:
Only one week to the dance. I can hardly wait. I wish I had something better to wear, but money is pretty tight around here. I asked Mom to give me some dancing lessons. I don't want to look like an oaf at the dance. Can A.S. dance? I'm not sure. I don't want M.B. dancing with that imbecile all evening.

Can you believe it, Dumb Diary? Entry after entry about the most **ridiculous things** you can imagine. All the important things she should be thinking about, all the meaningful things she could be saying, and she's all twisted up over some boy and some pretty girl that's making her jealous.

I should ask Hudson what he thinks about this sometime when Angeline isn't gorgeously leading him around by his eighth **(possibly seventh)** cutest nose.

SATURDAY 21

Dear Dumb Diary,

Hudson **called** here this morning before I was even awake. Back when I was dumber, I probably would have dumbly called him back right away to say something dumb, but those days are behind me now.

Or maybe — back in those dumb old days of mine — I would have called Isabella to see if she wanted to hang around and do **something dumb** like have a dance-off with my beagles, who can practically never beat us, except for that one time.

It may have been a little mean of me, but I have to say, nobody can **out-twerk** a beagle with a balloon tied to his tail. Scientists are certain that this is how twerking was invented in the first place.

Mom asked me if I wanted to go with her to drop off a picture of Grandma for framing. I wanted to, but I actually have a lot of homework this weekend and I needed to get started **pretending** that I was doing it.

Pretending to do homework is the first step to actually doing it.

STEP ONE: SHARPEN PENCILS

STEP TWO: SHARPEN MORE PENCILS

STEP THREE: TAKE HOMEWORK SELFIE

STEP FOUR: SHARPEN MORE PENCILS

SUNDAY 22

Dear Dumb Diary,

What the heck.

I hopped out of bed early this morning and **DID** my homework. Not **pretended** to do it. I **did it.** Like with actual pencils and words and numbers.

I know what you're thinking, Dumb Diary, but no, the TV was working fine.

And the Internet was functioning normally.

And the dogs didn't have **Diarrhoyal** on my bed again. (That's my medical term for a royal case of diarrhea.)

I just felt like maybe I need to be **smarter,** you know, for the sake of my granddaughter, who is surely reading my diary right now.

(You hear that, **Elialexithity**? Grandma here, not being dumb. And by the way, your name: Elialexithity is one I created by combining the three most beautiful names I know — Elizabeth, Felicity, and Alexandra.

So you're welcome.)

Elialexithity

Look! you get to do 3 HEARTS!

I also cleaned my room, and I didn't even use the method where you put everything in a drawer. It took me **hours** to do, and I found a sock that I remember losing in the third grade that has evidently been sitting here, on the floor, in plain sight for the entire time. I wonder why I didn't think of looking for it **on the floor**.

I brushed Stinker, too, and it may be the first time I ever did because I had enough hair to make a new Stinker. This interested him so much that while I was downstairs getting a broom, I believe he may have eaten his **hair twin**. I can't blame him. It was a **magnificent** thing to behold. I probably would have eaten mine.

I probably have enough hair stuck in my brushes to construct a HAIR JAMIE

Oh my gosh she would be like my beautiful beautiful baby

I even helped Mom with her special project today. Sometimes Mom likes to wreck a few dinners **in advance** on Sunday, and then freeze them for us to microwave during the week when there isn't enough time to wreck them from scratch.

It was the kind of **productive, meaningful** Sunday that you kind of wish your grandmother would have written about instead of this:

If I live to be a hundred years old, nothing will ever matter to me as much as this dance and making the right impression on M.B. I'm telling you, Diary, NOTHING.

Snap out of it, Granny! C'mon! Care about something smarter than this! Don't you know that you're not going to

Shouting in a DIARY

that works, right?

live forever.

Here's a list of the people who have.

Dear Dumb Diary,

Isabella was up in the library at lunch today, doing whatever it is she's doing on the computer these days. **She still won't talk about it.** Dicky got caught sneaking out of the lunchroom, trying to smuggle a lunch for her in his hat.

Bruntford got a confession out of him pretty easily — she was using that teacher grip where they're not really hurting you but you know they could if they wanted to. It's a grip they develop through years of opening countless **aspirin bottles**. Teachers eat those like salted peanuts.

Not much of a loss for Isabella anyway. I can't imagine what school macaroni marinated in Dicky's dirty little hat would taste like. Oh wait, yes I can:

NO DIFFERENT.

The DREADED TEACHER CLUTCH

Angeline sat down next to me while I was smartly eating kale. It's pretty much the only way you *can* eat it. Not happily, not enthusiastically, not attractively. Just smartly.

"You going to the dance?" she asked me.

"Not the best use of my time," I said **gagfully**, as the taste of the kale snuck up on me a little as I was talking.

I saw Angeline consider, just for a moment, putting her hand on mine. And then she changed her mind.

Her eyes were even bigger and more watery than ever. They were so watery that it actually started to feel a little humid around her face. I knew she wanted to say something kind and sensitive. **She's like that.**

I smiled at her.

"Hey, why don't you **fart off**?" I said sweetly.

Is that a thing? Telling somebody to **"fart off"**? I think it **must** be, because it seemed to have the desired effect on Angeline. She inhaled sharply, stood, and turned quickly, making her hair crack like a little whip.

Though, okay, there are probably **smarter** ways to say the same thing.

Could you please drift away gently on the breeze like a tiny fart?

Such sophistication

Because, you know, I'm all about the **smart** now.

TUESDAY 24

Dear Dumb Diary,

I read another entry from Grandma today.

My best friend, R., pointed out that I'm developing a blemish right in the middle of my forehead. I suppose I should be grateful to have it brought to my attention, but I could have done without the laughter. I'll have to see if the pharmacist can recommend something. I don't want to look like a Cyclops at the dance.

A.S., as you can imagine, has never been afflicted with a pimple or blemish or wart, and struts around with a complexion that looks like the finest satin cloth.

And like cloth, I might enjoy putting a few stitches in it.

I don't think Grandma should be talking about hitting little girls even if she was one.

Hudson Rivers stopped in front of my locker today. He didn't say anything at first, which made me think that something was **bothering** him.

I really wanted to know how to help. I wanted to find out what was wrong.

So I asked.

"What's your problem?" I said.

I immediately realized that I hadn't sounded as caring as I meant to, and I made a note to myself to sound **more caring** when I actually do care.

Then Hudson stood there, saying things about stuff.

Or maybe it was stuff about things.

I have no idea **what things** or **what stuff**, because it was one of those moments where neither his mouth nor my ears were trying very hard. It was only a matter of moments before our feet decided to move in different directions and the conversation was over.

I really think **spontaneous conversations** should be planned better.

Angeline is obviously **upset** with me now. She walked right past me at lunch today without saying hello, and I could tell that she wanted me to know that she was walking right past me, because she walked slowly and flipped a little shampoo fragrance my way, which is something she's always been capable of doing, but hasn't done at me for a **long time**.

She intentionally flipped green-apple fragrance at me even though we all know darn well she could have flipped something pleasant like vanilla. **Nope**, instead she chose the sourest fruit that people are still willing to eat.

It's a very subtle form of assault, but **I speak her language**.

Isabella wasn't at lunch — she's still busy with **whatever** in the library — so I ate with Dicky. I know I shouldn't mind, because I've learned that even though Dicky appears to be kind of deformed and a social mudpuddle, he actually has a huge heart and a lot of great things going for him, even though I found myself secretly wishing that there were **bees** going for him today instead.

He was making some sort of conversation but I wasn't paying attention, so I have to assume it was something about some **recently received wedgie.**

On occasion he also refers to these as **"melvins"** or **"getting mail"** — as in, "somebody put a letter in the slot." You've heard about Eskimos and snow. Nerds have over two hundred words for **Underwear Victimization.**

I found myself beginning to **wonder** if
all of middle school is just Hudson's stammering,
Angeline's hair-flipping, Dicky's wedgies, and
Isabella's whatever-it-is-she's-doing-in-the-library.
Maybe that's all it was for Grandma, too.

WEDNESDAY 25

Dear Dumb Diary,

Mom asked me about the dance at breakfast. My breakfast routine used to be like this:
Open fridge.
Find nothing to eat.
Close fridge.
Lower hopes.
Repeat.
But I'm smarter than that now, so today I had one of those important cereals that are full of meaningful ingredients. And since this stuff takes a lot of **force and time** to chew, I was at the table longer than usual.

"Are you going to that dance on Friday?" Mom asked.

I put up one finger in the **Universal Sign** for "Wait a second. I'm chewing. This garbage doesn't go down easy."

"You used to go to all the dances," she said. "I think you should go."

Huge gulpy noise like a donkey swallowing an ashtray.

I also sounded a little bit like a penguin swallowing a stapler

or maybe a koala swallowing a much larger koala

"I might, Mom," I finally replied, "but don't you think that school dances are kind of . . . **dumb**?"

My mom looked at me for a long time, and I got the impression that maybe she was thinking deeply about something.

"I don't think they are. But it's okay if you do," she said.

Sounds **innocent**, right? But I know this game.

Mom knows that sometimes I just say the opposite of whatever she says, because I can't help myself and I just need to argue with her. I don't know why I do it. Maybe she deserves it. I don't know.

But here, when she said, *"I don't think they are,"* she immediately added, *"But it's okay if you do."*

See? **NOW**, no matter what I say, I'll be agreeing with her, but also disagreeing with her. **Mom has a devious side.**

Arguing with Mom isn't something I like to do

It's more like something I Have to do

I still owed her an answer to her first question about going to the dance. I took another bite of "cereal" and chewed slowly. I needed a second to think before I spoke, but also if you don't chew healthy cereal slowly, you will vomit and die.

"I haven't decided yet," I said. Which is true. **At least as true as it needs to be.**

THURSDAY 26

Dear Dumb Diary,

Aunt Carol and Uncle Dan came over for dinner tonight. After dessert, Aunt Carol came up to my room. She wanted to know if I had had a chance to read through the diary that had been in the box.

"Oh, was there a diary in there?" I said, perfectly making her **totally believe** that I never saw it.

"I know you found it. Did you read it?" she asked.

"I may have glanced through a page or two," I said. "I don't think you can violate a person's privacy with **glances**."

A casual glance.

"I read **every single word**," Aunt Carol admitted, and she laughed this sinister little laugh like a girl version of that guy with knives on his fingers, except that she has really pretty polish on hers. "Amazing how some things never change, huh? In many ways we're all so much alike," she went on. "That could have been my diary, or your mom's. I'll bet you write stuff like that in yours."

And then I **exploded** a little.

"But everything she wrote was so **dumb**!" I said. "She's worried about all this stupid stuff! She wasted so much time worrying about nothing! **Doing** nothing. She was going to be somebody's grandma one day, but she doesn't write one single grandmotherly thing."

Aunt Carol looked a little confused, and then she started to laugh again.

"Of course there isn't anything **grandmotherly** in there!" she said. "It's not your **grandmother's** diary."

BLOWN

"It's your **grand*father*'s** diary," she added.

"**WAT**," I said.

And I said it just like that.

WAT.

I flipped through the pages. I thought back to the entries.

"But . . . she was talking about going to a dance . . . with M.B."

"**HE** was talking about going to a dance. M.B. stands for Mary Beth. Your grandpa was talking about your grandma. Her name was Mary Beth," she said, and I saw her eyes get all watery. "He fell in love with her in middle school."

I ran over and grabbed the picture of Grandpa — my big, tough, scary-looking grandpa.

"**THIS GUY** was all tied up in knots over a girl?"

HAIR SLICKED BACK WITH BLACK GREASE MADE FROM JUICED VAMPIRES

EYES CONFIDENT ENOUGH TO PERSUADE SHARKS, BEARS, AND POSSIBLY GRANDMAS

JAW SO MANLY THAT SMALL BOYS SPONTANEOUSLY SPROUT BEARDS JUST BY LOOKING AT IT

Aunt Carol gave the picture a big kiss.

"Of course! Guys feel the same things girls do. They get jealous, and hurt, and fall in love. Heck, your Uncle Dan cries at the sad parts in movies, but he pretends not to. He always blames it on allergies — allergies that only act up when the main character faces some kind of tragedy."

Hey, I think Isabella has allergies in movies sometimes.

Aunt Carol smiled. "In many of the ways that matter, Jamie, boys and girls are not so terribly **different**. It's just that some people don't always want to share what they're feeling."

FEELINGS-HIDERS: you are not as good at hiding as you think.

"No drawings," I said, suddenly aware of the absence. "There are no drawings in this diary. Grandma was a really good artist. I should have noticed that."

"I have to take the diary back now," Aunt Carol said. "I'm going to give it to your mom, and I don't want her to know that I gave it to you first."

I asked if she knew who A.S. was.

"A.S.?" she asked.

"That really handsome boy that Grandpa wrote about being jealous of. Beautiful hair. Maybe he also had a crush on Grandma?"

"Oh right. That was such a long time ago, Jamie. **Nobody in the world** could ever figure that mystery out."

He didn't really have a face like this. It's just how I show it's a mystery

After Aunt Carol left, I looked at my ugly necklace for a long time. All the dumb stuff in that diary totally **DID** matter.

It all added up to a **life**. The dumbness. The smartness. The extra-dumbness. The super-extra-dumbness.

The dance really and truly was the **most important thing**.

Oh my gosh.
Hudson.

FRIDAY 27

Dear Dumb Diary,

It's very difficult when your dumbness leaves you. You suddenly realize that, in some ways, your dumbness is your **best part**.

I found Hudson as quickly as I could and said the dumbest thing I could think of.

"Hey, Hudson. **Want to go to the dance with me?**" I dumbed.

He looked a little surprised and then smiled broadly.

"Yeah. Yes. Sure," he said. "But I got the feeling you weren't interested. I wanted to say something about your grandma, but every time I tried, you always just —"

I cut him off in midsentence.

But you know, adorably

"I know. I'm sorry. I was just not being dumb. It won't happen again. I'll be dumb from now on. Not totally dumb. Dumb enough. Not all the time. **Dumb when I should be.**"

And Hudson, incredibly, seemed to know what I meant.

Then I found Angeline.

"**I'll fix the posters.** Miss Anderson will let me work in the art room at lunch."

Angeline hugged me.

"I'm sorry," she said. "I shouldn't have —"

I cut her off in midsentence, too.

"I'm sorry, too, but remember, you and I aren't huggers, Ang. We talked about how some of us have our own **personal space** that we don't want filled with you, and I'm the queen of those people."

In the coils of a
BLONDACONDA

"And I'm fine. I'm fine now. Let me fix the posters," I said. **And I did.** I know it was a little late to do it, since they would only be up a few hours before the dance, but I felt like I had to fix them. I had to.

And the dance was great. Lots of balloons and decorations and music. I had a lot of fun, maybe for the first time in weeks. I think my grandpa and grandma would have liked how **dumb** it was.

But Isabella was looking a little sad, so I talked to her for a while out in the hall.

"I let you down, Jamie. **I let your grandma down**," she said.

"What are you talking about?"

When somebody who is ALWAYS sad gets even sadder, it's like if somebody gave you a garbage sandwich

And stepped on it first

"After we found out about your grandma's school, I started doing **research**. Even with those old vampire bats hovering around me in the library, I found records for everybody in her class.

"I looked in the records for any boy with the initials M.B. — remember, that was the boy she liked? — or any girl with the initials A.S. — the brunette that was making her life difficult.

"My plan was to find this A.S. and do something terrible to her lawn maybe, or egg her car, you know, as a kind of **sweet memorial** for your grandma.

"But I couldn't find a girl with the initials A.S. or a boy with the initials M.B."

I gave Isabella a gentle hug, which she almost always interprets as a deadly attack, but not this time.

LOOK! SHE EVEN SMILED!

OKAY NOT REALLY BUT I DIDN'T GET SLAPPED!

"It turns out it was my **grandpa's** diary. M.B. was my grandma," I said.

Isabella went all blank in the face. I could almost see her scanning the information inside her head. Then she grinned, and it was like a balloon **popped**. Maybe from the grin, maybe not. **Who can say?**

"So. A.S. was a boy," Isabella said, nodding. "In that case, I know **exactly** what to do."

Isabella has been known to make milk curdle with this grin

The next thing I knew, she had dragged me over to the refreshment table, where some of the teachers were handing out cookies and lemonade.

"Mr. Smith," she said. "Did you by any chance attend Walker Middle School in Hazel Heights? Or should I call you . . . **Algernon** Smith?"

Mr. Smith was so surprised I thought his toupee was going to spin right off the top of his head.

"How could you possibly know . . ." he sputtered, and Isabella pulled her leg back into the ready position. Mr. Smith was in greater danger than he knew. I've seen Isabella kick *chairs* between the legs so hard that they never stood correctly again.

I stepped protectively in front of him.

THE DREADED

READY POSITION

"Move, Jamie," Isabella said. "I'm doing this for your grandma. Although I guess that now I'm doing it for your grandpa. When I depart this world, I don't want to leave anybody **unkicked**. I just want for your grandpa what I would want for myself."

Mr. Smith put his hand on my shoulder. "I did go to Walker Middle School, and I knew your grandma," he said.

He knew my grandma. I really thought that Mr. Smith was less ancient than that. I guess that wig of his does kind of work.

WITH   WITHOUT

"She was beautiful, Jamie. Oh, I had a little crush on her. All the fellows did."

"She really **was** just like me," I said totally modestly.

"I knew your grandpa, too. He was tough as nails, a real tiger. Made out of iron. The two of them were perfect for each other. **I never stood a chance**," he said, and a look of sadness flickered across his face.

I heard the tendons in Isabella's legs untighten. She was considering not kicking Mr. Smith.

"I thought about telling you when I made the connection, Jamie, but I thought it might be weird for you."

Good call, Mr. Smith. Weird is exactly the word for that.

SOUND OF MUSCLES AND LIGAMENTS LOOSENING

I don't know how to write that so just imagine it.

"Anyway, I really am very sorry, Jamie. Your grandma is a great girl. Lots of laughs."

I took a breath.

IS.

Mr. Smith said **is**. And he called her a girl. Not a grandma, or an old lady. She's still there, alive, in his head, and in there, she's a girl.

"She liked your hair," I said. "And my grandpa was jealous of it."

He laughed and ran his fingers across his wig.

"I had that going for me, anyway," he said. "I only wear this ridiculous toupee to stay connected to those days. I know it's not fooling anybody."

"THAT'S A WIG?" I said, perfectly fooling him into thinking I believed it was real.

"Nice try," he said with a chuckle. "Your grandma was a terrible liar, too."

I took off the super-ugly necklace I'd found in my grandma's stuff and handed it to Mr. Smith.

"Could you please hang on to this for me while I'm dancing? I wouldn't want to **lose** it."

He looked down at it and he seemed hypnotized, transported to a time long ago, when grandmas and grandpas were kids with ugly necklaces and real hair, living in a world where you could buy anything for a quarter, and everybody had the same **dumb issues** they have now.

He smiled sweetly, and then Isabella **kicked** him.

DRAMATIZATION
DO NOT TRY THIS
AT HOME

It wasn't one of her regular kicks — I mean, her shoe stayed on and everything. And Mr. Smith didn't even go all the way down to the ground.

I explained to him why Isabella felt the need to do it — she was just trying to take care of some **unfinished business** for my grandpa.

He said he understood and wouldn't punish her for it.

"I'd like to think somebody might take care of my unfinished business one day," he said in a super-high voice.

"I might just do that," Isabella said, handing him his wig, which had landed on the oatmeal cookies.

As if Oatmeal Cookies weren't gross enough already

The rest of the dance was terrific. **And dumb.** I dumbly danced with Hudson, and then dumbly danced with Angeline, and we all dumbly danced with Dicky. He challenged Isabella to a dance-off, which he might have actually won, except that halfway through he started coughing up some wig hair that had accidentally gotten into his oatmeal cookies. **Huh.**

I honestly can't remember when I've had a **dumber** time.

SATURDAY 28

Dear Dumb Diary,

Mom got out Grandpa's diary this morning and we curled up on the couch and read parts of it together.

She had never read it before, and when I told her how surprised I was that Grandpa was kind of a **big, fluffy bunny** when it came to Grandma, she said that Dad was the same way.

"Your dad cried during *Bambi*," Mom said. "I didn't want him to feel weird about it, so I had to cry, too. I just thought about my favorite shoes getting ruined."

We looked through the diary and she really and truly cried and laughed, and then I cried and laughed, too. In the end, I think she laughed more than she cried, and she even started **snorting and cackling** like she used to. I think it might have been Grandpa's dumbness that really helped her the most.

She seemed less like a little girl that had lost her mom forever, and more like a little girl that would never lose her mom again.

I was amazed at how much I liked the sound of her laugh

Later on, I started thinking back on all the things I've done — the smart things, the dumb things, the super-dumb things, the extra-super-dumb things — and I realized that often the **dumb things** lead me to something smart.

It's not that smartness is bad. Smartness is critical, but it's like dumbness is this magical thing. At first you resent and regret it, but eventually, you realize you need it in order to get to the smart part.

And maybe sometimes the dumbness is even the best part of your day. Or your week. **Or your life.**

I never should have tried to abandon it. I really thought it was a change for the better, but I think sometimes it's actually better to **change for the worse.**

Thanks for listening, Dumb Diary,

Jamie Kelly

How Dumb Can You Be?

Jamie tries to live each day to the dumbest — but can *you*? Try to choose the dumbest response to each situation below!

1.) Your crush asks you to the school dance. You:
  a. Smile and say, "Have your people call my people and we'll set it up."
  b. Look at the floor and mumble, "Sure."
  c. Point down the hall and shout, "Whoa, is that a koala in a top hat?" and then run in the other direction before you have to say anything else.

2.) Your mom tells you to clean your room. What do you do?
   a. Shove everything in the closet and announce that you're done.
   b. Start cleaning, but get distracted by painting your dog's toenails.
   c. Tell her that if it's your room, you get to decide what it looks like, and if it's not your room, the owner should have to clean it.

3.) It's school picture day . . . but you spill juice on your favorite sweater on the way to school. What do you do?
   a. Keep the sweater on. Your mom will flip when she sees the picture!
   b. Shove the sweater in your locker and have your picture taken in the slightly less dirty T-shirt you wore underneath.
   c. Run to the cafeteria and spill everything you can find on your sweater. Now it looks like modern art!

4.) Your crazy aunt is coming to visit, and she's staying in your room while you sleep on the couch. What do you do?
a. Booby-trap your room and pretend you have no idea why she's covered with mustard and glitter when she comes out.
b. Grin and bear it. It's only for a few days, and at least you can make fun of her behind her back.
c. Feed your dog a half-dozen bean burritos and laugh as you watch him curl up at the foot of her bed to sleep.

5.) You're on vacation with your family, but your bag got lost at the airport. What's your plan?
a. Grab any other bag. Something will fit.
b. See how many different ways you can use the T-shirt, jeans, sweater, and jacket you wore on the plane. Jacket pants? Jeans on the head? The possibilities are endless!
c. Wear some of your mom's extra stuff, even though it's way too big. At least you're not around anyone you know! (And "accidentally" break the camera, just to make sure there's no photo evidence.)

6.) The sixth cutest guy in your grade sits down at your lunch table. You:
   a. Tell him it costs a dollar to sit there.
   b. Faint. This is sometimes for the best.
   c. Try not to blind him with your most charming smile.

7.) You have a big math test coming up. How do you prepare?
   a. Make up fabulous song and dance numbers to help you memorize your times tables. No one will mind if you have to do them during the test.
   b. Study all night, and then accidentally fall asleep the minute the test is passed out.
   c. Look over your notes a few times and hope for the best.

8.) The most perfectly perfect girl in school assaults you with a hair flip of her signature shampoo fragrance. You:
   a. Gasp and fall to the ground, choking.
   b. Try to hold your breath.
   c. Spray her with a bottle of your own concoction that you keep in your backpack for just such an occasion.

1.) a 2.) b 3.) c 4.) a OR c 5.) b 6.) b 7.) a 8.) c

Make Your Own Dumb Posters

Making school posters isn't for amateurs! Sketch some posters advertising the teams and events below. (Feel free to add as much glitter as you dare.)

Mathletes: Just like athletes, but not in any way fun to watch!

Join the soccer team!
Considered a sport in several countries.

Wherefore art thou, old-timey actors? Don't miss the Drama Club auditions for *Romeo and Juliet*!

Winter Carnival — making hypothermia fun again!

School Mascot Needed!
Qualifications: enthusiasm, ability to cartwheel and breathe under forty pounds of felt

Join the Cooking Club!
Hey, try not to accidentally poison anyone, okay?

My Dumb Family

Adults aren't immune to dumbness! Talk to the grown-ups in your life to find out the answers to the questions below. (Then hold the information over them forever!) What would they have written in their diaries afterward? Make up dumb diary entries for each one!

What's the dumbest thing your mom ever did?

_____

Write her fake diary entry about it here:

_____

_____

_____

_____

What's the dumbest thing your dad ever did?

_____

Write his fake diary entry about it here:

_____

_____

_____

_____

_____

_____

What's the dumbest thing your grandparents ever did?

_____

Write a fake diary entry about it here:

_____

_____

_____

_____

_____

DEAR DUMB DIARY,

CAN'T GET ENOUGH OF JAMIE KELLY?
CHECK OUT HER OTHER DEAR DUMB DIARY BOOKS!

YEAR TWO: #1: School. Hasn't This Gone On Long Enough?

YEAR TWO: #2: The Super-Nice Are Super-Annoying

YEAR TWO: #3: Nobody's Perfect. I'm As Close As It Gets.

YEAR TWO: #4: What I Don't Know Might Hurt Me

YEAR TWO: #5: You Can Bet On That

WWW.SCHOLASTIC.COM/DEARDUMBDIARY

#1: Let's Pretend This
Never Happened

#2: My Pants Are
Haunted!

#3: Am I the Princess or
the Frog?

#4: Never Do
Anything, Ever

#5: Can Adults Become
Human?

#6: The Problem With Here
Is That It's Where I'm From

#7: Never Underestimate
Your Dumbness

#8: It's Not My Fault I
Know Everything

#9: That's What Friends
<u>Aren't</u> For

#10: The Worst Things In
Life Are Also Free

#11: Okay, So Maybe I Do
Have Superpowers

#12: Me! (Just Like You,
Only Better)

Our Dumb Diary:
A Journal to Share

Totally Not Boring
School Planner

Don't miss the book that started it all — Jamie Kelly's very first diary!

Turn the page to sneak a peek inside the first diary of Jamie Kelly, who promises that everything she writes is true . . . or at least as true as it needs to be.

(But Jamie has no idea that anybody is reading her diaries — so please, please, please don't tell her.)

Dear Dumb Diary,

Today Hudson Rivers (eighth cutest guy in my grade) talked to me in the hall. Normally, this would have no effect on me at all, since there is still a chance that Cute Guys One Through Seven might actually talk to me one day. But when Hudson said, "Hey," today, I could tell that he was totally in love with me, and I felt that I had an obligation to be irresistible for his benefit.

So just as I'm about to say something cool back to Hudson (Maybe even something REALLY cool. We'll never know for sure now.), Angeline comes around the corner with her jillion cute things dangling from her backpack, and intentionally looks cute RIGHT IN FRONT OF HIS EYES. This scorpion-like behavior on her part made me forget what I was going to say, so the only thing that came out of my mouth was a gush of air without any words in it. Not like this mattered, because he was staring at Angeline the same way Stinker was staring at the ball a couple days ago.

STINKER   HUDSON

Confectionately Yours

Don't miss all the books in this delicious series!

Four girls, one charm bracelet, and a little bit of luck . . .

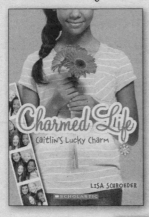

Charmed Life
Caitlin's Lucky Charm

LISA SCHROEDER

Charmed Life
Mia's Golden Bird

LISA SCHROEDER

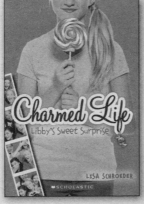

Charmed Life
Libby's Sweet Surprise

LISA SCHROEDER

Charmed Life
Hannah's Bright Star

LISA SCHROEDER

From the author of *It's Raining Cupcakes* comes a charming series about how anything is possible when you have great friends!

Some guys just can't win...but Danny never stops trying!

SCHOLASTIC and associated logos are trademarks and/or registered trademarks of Scholastic Inc.

SCHOLASTIC
scholastic.com

Available in print and eBook editions

LOSERLIST4e

Graphic novels by #1 *New York Times* bestselling author
Raina Telgemeier

This is the true story of how Raina severely injured her two front teeth when she was in the sixth grade, and the dental drama – on top of boy confusion, a major earthquake, and friends who turn out to be not so friendly – that followed!

Callie is the set designer for her middle school's spring musical, and is determined to create a set worthy of Broadway. But between the onstage AND offstage drama that occurs once the actors are chosen, it's going to be a long way until opening night!

ARE YOU YETI FOR ADVENTURE?

Join Blizz Richards as he keeps the world safe for goblins, sea monsters, unicorns, and Bigfeet of all kinds!

"Charming characters, hilarious illustrations, and a big bunch of fun!"
—Dav Pilkey, creator of Captain Underpants

SCHOLASTIC

SCHOLASTIC and associated logos are trademarks and/or registered trademarks of Scholastic Inc.

scholastic.com

YETI2A

About Jim Benton

Jim Benton is not a middle-school girl, but do not hold that against him. He has managed to make a living out of being funny, anyway.

He is the creator of many licensed properties, some for big kids, some for little kids, and some for grown-ups who, frankly, are probably behaving like little kids.

You may already know his properties: It's Happy Bunny™ or Catwad™, and of course you already know about Dear Dumb Diary.

He's created a kids' TV series, designed clothing, and written books.

Jim Benton lives in Michigan with his spectacular wife and kids. They do not have a dog, and they especially do not have a vengeful beagle. This is his first series for Scholastic.

Jamie Kelly has no idea that Jim Benton, or you, or anybody is reading her diaries. So, please, please, please don't tell her.